Gahan Wilson's Still Weird

FORGE

A Tom Doherty Associates Book
New York

STILL WEIRD

Some of the material in this book has appeared previously in one or more of the following publications: "... and then we'll get him!", Gahan Wilson's America, Gahan Wilson's Cracked Cosmos, Gahan Wilson's Graveside Manner, I Paint What I See, Is Nothing Sacred?, The Man in the Cannibal Pot, Playboy's Gahan Wilson, The Weird World of Gahan Wilson, Playboy, and The New Yorker.

This book is printed on acid-free paper.

A Forge Book
Published by Tom Doherty Associates, Inc.
175 Fifth Avenue
New York, N.Y. 10010

Design by Susan Hood

Library of Congress Cataloging-in-Publication Data

Wilson, Gahan.
    Still weird / Gahan Wilson.
      p.   cm.
    "A Tom Doherty Associates book."
    ISBN 0-312-85779-9 (pbk.)
    ISBN 0-312-85290-8 (hard)
      1. American wit and humor, Pictorial.   I. Title.
    NC1429.W5785A4   1994
    741.5'973—dc20   94-32370
                                            CIP

First edition: December 1994

Printed in the United States of America

0 9 8 7 6 5 4 3 2 1

"Face it, Edwin—it isn't that we've all turned into teddy bears,
it's that you've gone crazy!"

"He's programmed to take me home the minute
I start quoting Nietzsche."

"What's wrong with that damned kid?"

"Yes, it *is* a beautiful view, isn't it?"

"Can't we just go after striped bass or something like that?"

"It's the man from the gun lobby, Senator."

"Don't be afraid, dear—it's a tree!"

9

"Here's my plan. . . ."

"You never know what will catch on!"

". . . Well, I couldn't *believe* I'd actually got them eating *corn*, right? But there they were, *doing* it! So I figured, what the hell! Why not try it? And I said, 'Hey—you people ever thought of having a *turkey* for dinner?'"

"Spiders just can't resist Harry!"

"Oh, shut up, Johnson. We'll go back to using puppies the second they send us some more!"

SALESMEN RING HERE

SALESMEN RING HERE

". . . and this looks like a tiny pair
of aqualungs!"

"You mean you have survived the last seventeen years
on a diet of little green lizards?"

"Take it from me, buddy—at seventy-five score
and ten it's a steal."

"You spit out Dr. Harper this very minute!"

"All right, then—*now* what are you going to do?"

"What the hell, sweetheart—if you want it, it's yours!"

"Okay, now put Tab A into Slot B."

"He just loves his cute little postmortem doll!"

"I figure everybody else is doing it."

"See what I mean? No matter how many times I pull
its trigger, the damned thing just won't fire!"

"Big deal!"

"Do you ever catch yourself wondering if all this is only
part of some crazy experiment?"

"You really miss her, don't you, Lou?"

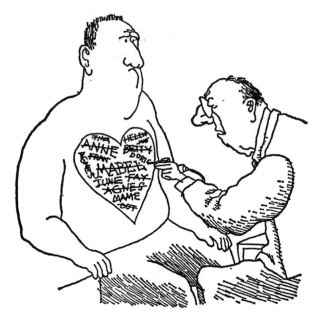

"This girl had better be it, young man!"

"I'm over here, you fool!"

"The Boston Strangler!"
"Frankenstein Meets the Wolfman?"
"Breathless?"
"Something by Shakespeare?"

"When did you first become aware of this imagined 'plot
to get you,' Mr. Potter?"

"Things really get a little crazy here
around Mother's Day!"

"Oh, I bet he's the fellow who's in all the papers!"

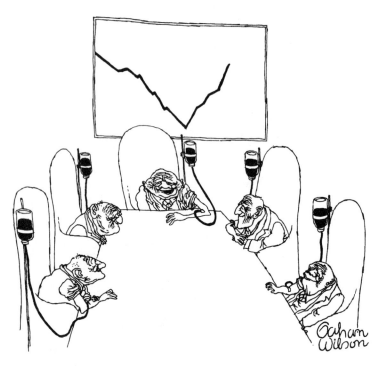

"I've said all along this firm just needed
a little new blood!"

"Life is like . . . ah . . . life is . . . uhm . . . like . . . er . . .
life is like a dream!"

"Uh—Carstairs—I've found something that may come as quite a surprise to the foundation!"

"Kill!"

"This *is* the toy department, sir!"

"How did you come to name your boat the *Revenge*, Captain?"

"Wrong door!"

"I suppose you've all been wondering why the corporation's called this little do a 'termination party.'"

"Congratulations, Ecological Disaster—it's not often we admit another horseman into the Apocalypse!"

"So far, all the tests indicate, as we feared, that you *are* a cocker spaniel."

"Amazing, what they can do
with plastic."

"So hey, is that as cute as a button or what?"

"I'm afraid this town has gotten to be just a
little too tough for super heroes!"

"Here's his left foot."

"Oh, sir—we local folk never ever looks
into the pond!"

"Your place is back out there on the lawn, buddy!"

"I think it means we'd better find some shade!"

40

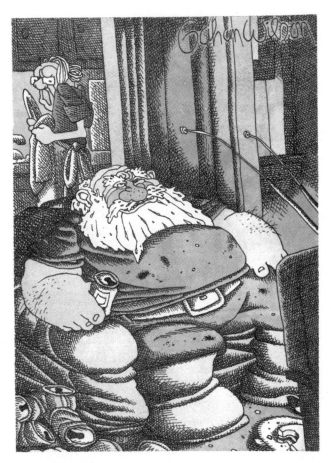

"I just pray to God that none of those poor, dear, innocent children ever see you when you get like this!"

"Having fun, kids?"

"It's just something that's going around."

"In a strange way, General, we may have brought all this upon ourselves!"

"Wow! Wait'll I tell Dr. Feldman about
this dream!"

"You can tell she's thinking it over."

"First, let me put your mind at ease about that being a hallucination. . . ."

"For heaven's sake—why can't you leave me alone?"

"Somehow I thought the whole thing would
be a lot classier!"

"Thank heaven they're finally starting to worry about the greenhouse effect!"

"Did you or did you not employ a leash to drag your cairn terrier, Jack, away from the corner of Park Avenue and Sixty-fifth Street in spite of his making every effort to clearly indicate to you that he wished to stay where he was?"

"Well, we found out what's been clogging up your drains!"

"Talk about your cut-rate operations. . . ."

"It's a lot more fun this way, isn't it?"

READ IT NOW!

THE TRUTH ABOUT SAUCERS

ONLY $6.00 AT YOUR LOCAL BOOKSTORE

"Whoever they are, they've sold out."

"I don't know how we ever got along
without the stuff."

"Harry, I really think you ought to go to the doctor."

"Good grief—he's writing out Lucile!"

"You're not telling Mr. Bennett what he wants to hear!"

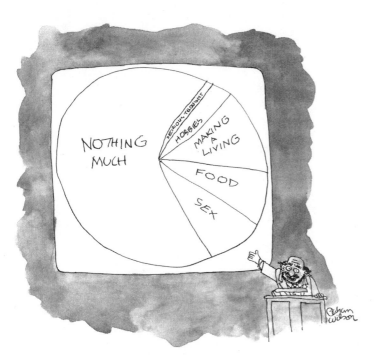

"Of course, this is only an ideal for which we strive!"

"No fair turning yourself off, Mr. Hasbrow!"

". . . If I might have Your Honor's
undivided attention?"

"How did a guy like you ever get
into a business like this?"

"Er, driver, just let me off right here, please!"

"It strikes me you've made a great deal of bother over
very little, Baskerville."

"How do you suppose young Ainsworth's
so damned sharp at spotting tombs?"

"Okay, remember, now—you're this giant."

"Very well, Miss Apple—call my broker."

"Hey, Mac, which way to the
Tall Girls Boutique?"

"Anyhow, the article in the *Times* says they were only hibernating and the greenhouse effect has brought them out."

"Wonderful! This way I can go block after block talking to myself and nobody looks at me as if I were crazy."

"They didn't *used* to behave like that!"

"It's been awful for business, Mrs. Schultz, but it was Charlie's last wish."

"Yes, I must admit I've done rather well here."

"And you, sir—have you a request
for our strolling whistler?"

"Over there."

"Of course, it doesn't pay as much
as during the season."

"Surprise!"

"Harriet? You'll never guess who's here!"

"Sorry to keep you so late, but I'm determined to get to the bottom of this werewolf fixation of yours."

"That's a cloud, too. They're all clouds."

"Jesus Christ, Sergeant—what the hell kind of place *is* this?"

1.

2.

3.

Gahan Wilson

"I *love* it!"

"All this fuss and bother just because of a
damned heart attack!"

"One day, when he's old and feeble, he'll be in a nostalgic mood, and he'll come up here to see us again, and to reminisce—*and then we'll get him!*"

"Tell him I'm still busy and put him on hold
again with that horrible music!"

"The hell with *this* stuff!"

"Easy on the fast balls, will you, kid?"

"That is not the mood we're trying to get across
out here, Parker!"

"I knew you'd be happy here, Weslie!"

"I can't understand why we always have
such awful luck getting a cab!"

"Harry always said genetic engineering would be a big mistake!"

Gahan Wilson

". . . Only a minute or so more and man will have his first view of the other side of the moon!"

"Strange, my missing wife also complained about having an enormous tank of piranha in the living room!"

"Ah, well—back to business."

"Funny thing. Eddie was always sure a
meteor would get him."

"This is *not* going to help my messianic complex, Doctor."

"Well, it's certainly no one *I* know!"

"Thank God!"

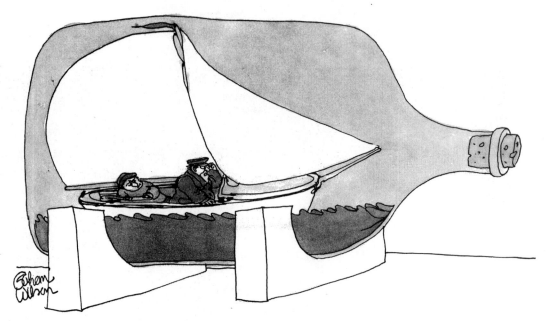

"This is getting us nowhere!"

"Ding dong the witch is dead!"

"Looking good, Larry!"

"Then, after you have spent those thirty years working
your heart out on the company's production line, you will
be laid off because of a corporate merger, only to discover
you have lost all your retirement benefits."

"Get back! Get back!"

"Happy New Year!"

"The doctors . . . say . . . they've never . . . seen . . . another case quite like it."

"Somehow, somewhere along the line, this town lost its pride."

"There you are, you naughties!"

"I'm afraid all we can do is operate and hope they
don't continue to spread!"

"I'm Special Agent Kerrington, of the FBI, Mr. Ently, and I just wanted you to know that we've checked you out and you're a good citizen."

"Thank you. And my friend's is made of rough
canvas and has leather straps sewn into it."

"Oh, yes, and that's another thing, Mrs. Salzman. Don't do
that anymore to Mr. Salzman."

"Yeah? Well, they don't make *me* feel
insignificant, fella!"

"Of course he eats like a horse—what in
God's name did you expect?"

"What's that, kid? I can't make out what
you're trying to say."

"I paint what I see, child."

"Of course, the place wouldn't seem so small if we weren't elephants."

"Is nothing sacred?"

"We may already be too late, Mr. Parker."

"Frankly, I think you'd be well advised
not to get a dog, sir."

"This is Willy, and this is Willy's
imaginary playmate."

"I don't know, man—sometimes I feel
you're wrong for the movement!"

"Sorry I'm not making myself clearer, but it's hard to express yourself in a language as crude and primitive as ours."

"Matilda, you've forgotten to dust Mr. Harper!"

"It happens."

"You'd better adjust that freezer."

"To the lunatic fringe!"

"I tell you, Mr. Arthur, this survey has no way
of registering a nonverbal response!"

"I *thought* he seemed depressed!"

"Watch out for the fourth step."

"Look—you can see where I carved my initials into his shell when I was a kid!"

"I'll take *that* one!"

"When will you accept it, Hallahan?
I *am* holier than thou."

"He owed me a month's wages when he died,
and he's going to work it out."

"Of course I'm always careful to keep the TV set turned on!"

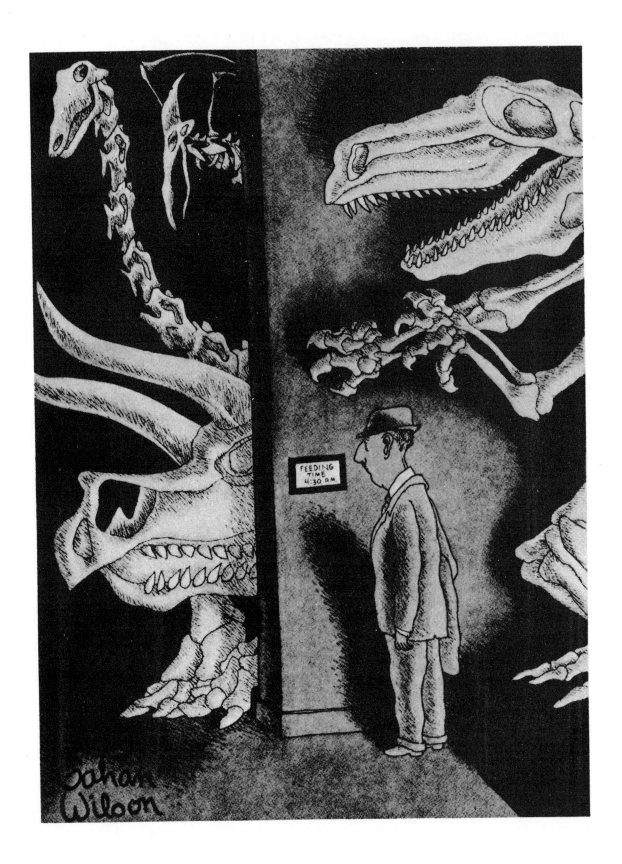

"Your Honor, the defense contends its client could never get a fair trial in this court."

"Ed! Run! It's a trap!"

"And now may I bite your neck?"

119

"God only knows where he bags them."

"Name your poison."

"It's so pleasant to watch a man who really
enjoys his work!"

"You use inferior materials, you get inferior demons."

"Look—I may just be a recorded message, but that doesn't give you the right to talk to me that way!"

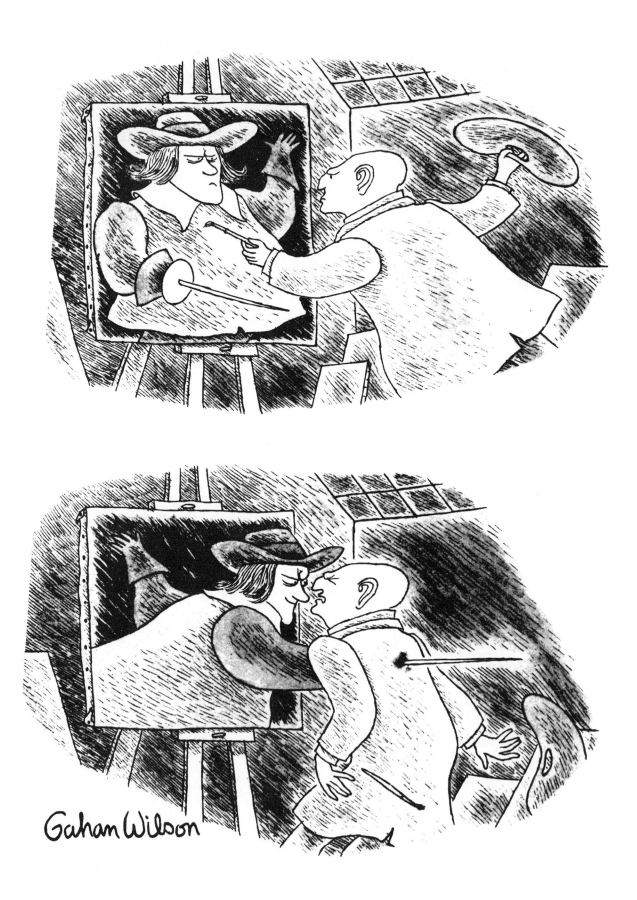

Gahan Wilson

"Floor, please."

"Looks like we can't expect to find much in that direction."

BEWARE
OF OWNER

"Surely we can't have been *meant* for
drudgery such as this!"

"Oh, *relax*, for God's sake!"

"Can't we just go after sailfish . . . ?"

"Well, now—what seems to be the trouble?"

". . . But enough of shop talk . . ."

"Of course you understand I'm very, *very* glad they've brought back the wolves!"

"It's a forgery—and a recent one, too."

"Oh, grow up, Jack!"

"You're right—this scene *did* call for a stunt man!"

"Now, George, if our Harry wants to dedicate his life to
fighting evildoers and upholding the forces of law and
order, I don't think we should stand in his way!"

"I think we're in real trouble!"

"You're fired, Mysto!"

"Just watching faces in the fire, pet."

"He hasn't been the same since George died."

"Oh, God—now here go the people from downstairs!"

"I don't know, Professor, this civilization is so primitive,
it hardly seems worth our time!"

"Of course, once the plague's done, we're both out of a job."

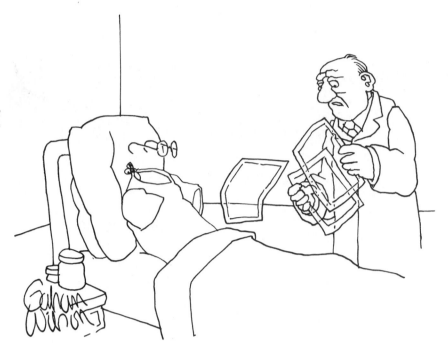

"Looks like your X-rays are just more of the same, Mr. Jennings."

"It looks like we can't expect much in the
way of benign guidance."

"Here it comes!"

"Fred, I think you're spending altogether too much time down
here with these mushrooms!"

"... is pleased to announce a complete and devastating victory over the enemy.
This is a recorded message. The government is pleased ..."

"Now exactly at what hour of the evening of December the twenty-fourth did Professor Pohlman query you as to the best method of killing Miss Burkhardt?"

"You know very well you're not supposed
to beg at the table!"

"Excuse me for shouting—I thought
you were farther away."

"I'd say it's a pretty obvious case of evolution
taking a wrong turn."

"Well, we found out what's been clogging your chimney since last December, Miss Emmy."

145

"Look—I've really *got* to leave!"

"I'm afraid we have a skeptic among us. . . ."

"I'm sorry—where was I?"

"I'll talk! I'll TALK!"

"Take it from me, Mr. Kirby—you're an
ear, nose and throat man's dream."

"I'm far from done, you fool!"

"This preparation will eliminate fleas, this one ticks,
this one various other vermin and considerable fungi,
and this one will eliminate the dog itself."

"Something's gone horribly wrong with the copying machine!"

"Then Mrs. Cratchit entered, smiling proudly, with the pudding. Oh, a wonderful pudding! Shaped like a cannonball, blazing in half a quartern of ignited brandy bedight with Christmas holly stuck into the top, and stuffed full with plums and sweetmeats and sodium diacetate and monoglyceride and potassium bromate and aluminum phosphate and calcium phosphate monobasic and chloromine T and aluminum potassium sulfate and calcium propionate and sodium alginate and butylated hydroxyanisole and . . ."

"I think I can speak for an entire generation when I say
I'm either in my thirties or in my forties."

"There're damned few who can walk away!"

"So when did you start up your collection, Mrs. Fennerman?"

"Harry!"

"Oh, go away!"

"Since there are no dissenting votes, let the minutes read that I am once again elected chairman of the board and granted another raise in salary."

"I've tried to make it as authentic as I could!"

"Good lord, Holmes! How did you come to know
I'd seafood for lunch?"

"Best damn special effects man in
the business!"

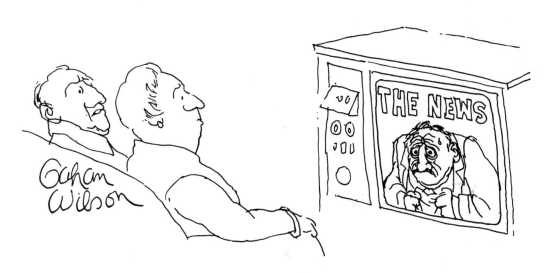

"My God—it must really be bad tonight!"

"Sorry, son, but from now on you're classified."

"I am sorry, ma'am, but this is really very much out of my line."

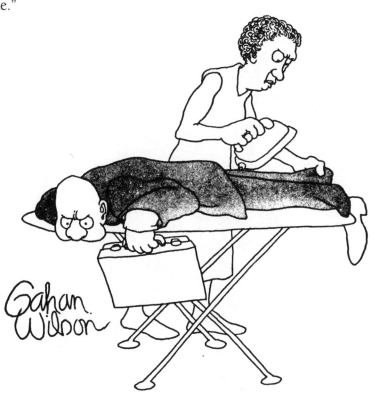

"Wait a minute. There's another little wrinkly spot over here."

"Here comes another!"

"Fetch!"

Gahan Wilson

"Look like nice folks—"

"Professor Zlata! You're just in time to be the planet Neptune!"

"Don't get it wrong, Bridget—the sacrifice of a white
rooster every third day at precisely high noon
without fail!"

"... but then I realized in order to make it work I'd have to invent a socket and God knows what else."

"Hold it, Charlie."

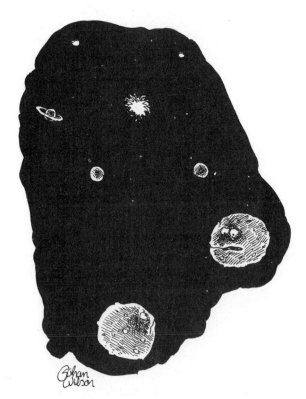

"I'm starting to suspect those things orbiting closer in are just hunks of minerals!"

"I've always *known* R.H. would be able to do that!"

"Have you been mean to Mr. Chair?"

"You know, Larry, with a smart lawyer
you could make a lot of money!"

"I think we've located the cause of that tie-up at Thirty-fourth Street and Seventh Avenue!"

"Gee—it's just like in the movies!"

"She's just *toying* with you, Parker!"

"We're not going to get anywhere with
this guy until sunrise."

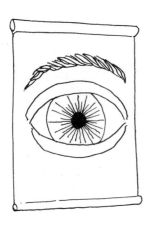

"*Well, now—what do you think of what Mr. Id just said, Mr. Super Ego?*"

"Now that you've come of age, son, I think it's time your old dad let you in on our little family curse."

"His first?"

"Basically, we're all trying to say the same thing."

"I wish you'd have a repairman fix it—
it's really getting on my nerves!"

"Never mind, Nurse, I've spotted the boy!"

"Damn it, Ferguson—grit your teeth and *cut!*"

"Dump all my shares of Peabody and Fenner!"

"Of course, there's always Planet Earth."

"I think she heard us!"

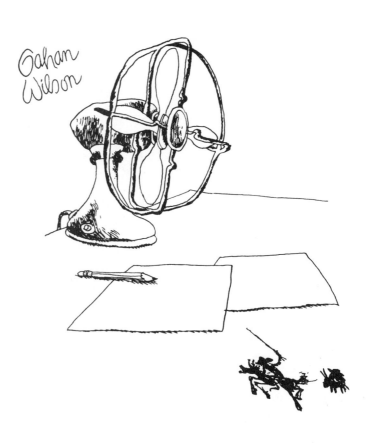

"Is it a straight drop to the street?"

"You're right—there *is* a letter 'G' in the verdict!"

"Can't we all stop squabbling?"

"It sure is great to be back in France."

"Whoops—*sorry*!!!"

"I'm afraid that tour's already fully booked!"

"Harry, this is turning out to be kind of
a creepy vacation!"

"Relax—all I want is a good table."

"Oh, yeah—we have lots of trouble with that one!"

"I should say this takes care of your 'intelligent
life on Earth' theory."

"I'll just take a half dozen since they're super jumbo."

"Of course you realize this may
be a difficult birth."

"Okay. Turn on the sprinkler."

"Damn it—I *told* them I was too well known for undercover work!"

"Women!"

"There will be an enormous fly in your future!"

"For God's sake, man—do your part and
bolt the stuff down!"

"My husband, of course, will want a den."

"Is this yours?"

"We are highly pleased at the negative comments
by your former employer!"

"Let's get out of here—this place is driving me crazy!"
"Let's get out of here—this place is driving me crazy!"
"Let's get out of here—this place is driving me crazy!"
"Let's get out of here—this place is driving me crazy!"
"Let's get out of here—this place is driving me crazy!"

"Watch out—it may be dangerous!"

"She sure has big teeth for such a little old lady!"

"I can remember when that sort of thing meant a lot to me!"

"I'll have some of what he's having!"

"The first time I saw you I knew you were the girl for me!"

"Have you considered installing a dehumidifier?"

". . . but I'd forgotten that you've had him
executed, haven't you?"

"I *told* you not to do that!"

"Come on, folks—let's see if we can't bring him back for just one more commandment!"

"What have you done *now*, Willy Smith?"

"You are Lieutenant Phil Reardon of the Bunco
Squad and are trying to nail me for fraud, but you
will fail."

"Gee, I can even remember back to when you could eat them."

"Would you care to step out of the shop and see how it looks
in the fog, Mr. Holmes?"

"Let's try and get through this autopsy, okay?"

"Accursed daylight saving time!"

"Oh, you see both sides to *everything*!"

"Good heavens—this must mean we've practically
finished him off!"

"*Damn*—stepped on another one of them!"

"Of course, their programming's not aimed at us!"

"I'll let you have one when you're not crazy."

"Keep chuckling. He has a way of suddenly
stepping back into the room."

217

"Sir! The Moorne Castle Monster is under the strict protection of the National Historical Trust!"

"What's say we evolve into land animals!"

"I just can't seem to get myself
organized this morning!"

"I don't like the looks of this!"

"I think I've found the trouble, Mr. Nadler!"

"But then summer's always tough!"

"I do wish you'd get over this morbid fear of spiders!"

"I'm afraid it was a pretty bad year all around."

"Later."

"My goodness, Mr. Merryweather, we certainly *did* make a boo-boo with that prescription of yours!"

"I think we have just the thing for
that upset tummy of yours,
Mrs. Starbright. . . ."

"Beat it, Mac—this entourage is complete!"

"Why—you're kind of cute!"

"Mind if we play through?"

"The map ends here, too!"

"I have to say they managed to cause a lot of damage for
such a short-lived species."

"Okay, you've had your look. Now bug off."

"I'm sorry, madam, but these units are
for display purposes only."

"The place hasn't been the same since that hole in the ozone opened up!"

"The one to the far right happens to be my own personal flag."

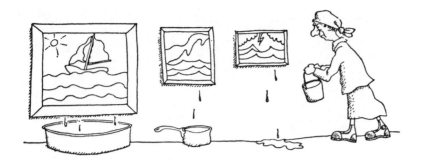

"... And if they won't do it for me then strike them dead with a lightning bolt like you did with Uncle Sherman."

"We've got to lighten up those fortune cookies!"

"I keep telling them to use sun block."

"Come over here, fellows—I think I've found
the solution to our problem!"

"It's me!"

"What do you say we give Chief Wapapatame here another of those Thanksgiving punches before talking over that little land deal?"

239

"Oh, Irwin, I wish to God you'd get rid of that thing!"

"Harry, I wish you'd stop *doing* that!"

"Extraordinary thing, Watson—the clues indicate the killer to have been a man of your exact build and appearance!"

"I think it's his beeper."

"The whole thing's much smaller than
it seemed on TV."

"Most emphatic rejection of foreign tissue I've ever seen!"

"I'm sorry, sir, but Professor Dornley does not wish to be
disturbed for the duration of the winter."

"Honestly, Harry, I'll never tease you again for carrying
around that elephant gun!"

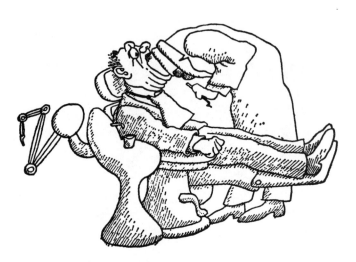

"Yes, sir, that back molar's got to go!"

"I can't tell you how relieved I was the first
time I saw you during the full moon!"

"To get to the main highway? Take the first left, turn along the hill till you get to the Devil's mouth."

"Wait 'til it gets a little closer!"

"He hasn't touched a thing for weeks!"

"Jeez, did *we* ever goof!"

"Here, puss, puss, puss!"

"Didn't work out, eh?"

"Well, Sam, baby, you pulled it off—the biggest deal of them all!"

"I wish you wouldn't worry so much about me, George.
After all, I'm only a figment of your imagination."

"It's for you, Muhammad!"

"Dr. Kreuger—what are you doing in
my recurrent nightmare?"

"I'b sorry I'b gibing you this horribo co'd."

"It's that bug that's been going
around town."

"Come on, Charlie, let me in on when you
guys are making the break!"

"Harry! *You?*"

"This isn't going to help, Edward."

"What are these funny black things you've sewn onto your sleeves, Edwin?"

"Oh, for heaven's sake, Fenner—let the chips fall where they may!"

"It's a break!"

"You rang, sir?"

"You're supposed to push your envelope from
the *inside*, Conners!"

"I'd say in that outfit you can handle just about anything Mother Nature dishes out, Mr. Harper!"

"The set you ordered arrived today, sir!"

"Enough yin. More yang."

"One small step for a znargh—a giant stride
for znarghkind!"

"... And just what do you think you're going to do with your silly death ray once you've finished it?!"

"One B.L.T., one cherry pie, and one bowl of
chili with crackers on the side!"

"While we've got the chance, Dad, we'd like to thank you
for these little glimpses of you we've had through the
years!"

"I suppose it was bound to happen."

"Get me God again, Miss Parker."

"Good lord, Holmes—you *are* a master of disguise!"

"The sky looks blue because your protective
lenses are tinted, dear."

"Let's hope that with the passage of time the human race will become three-dimensional."

"It's over, Harry!"

"Here's someone new for you to play with!"

"Young Brewster's really coming along, isn't he?"

"Now if the FDA doesn't tumble to us,
we'll make a bundle!"

"It was years before I realized they don't really need me after
a certain number of drinks."

"Yes, these will do nicely."

"Only mushrooms—no toadstools or footstools!"

"Kill!"

"I take it, Senator, you approve of
the present seniority system."

"You've got to come over at once, sir!
Something terrible's happening in the
hall of eggs!"

"You're putting in too many people!"

"Well? What's your excuse *this* time?"

"And to those of you who *did* contribute to the church fund—our blessings."

"Too bad—the kid had talent."

"I'm afraid you got the wrong Martin Barker."

"The place has sure changed!"

"So, did you hear about all the excitement?"

"Look—who needs you?"

"Please, George . . . not here!"

"I *thought* I was in particularly good form!"

"And every day it's costing more and more!"

1.

2.

Gahan
Wilson

GAHAN WILSON

Gahan Wilson is descended from P. T. Barnum and William Jennings Bryan, which may explain quite a bit about his sense of humor. He was officially born dead, which also probably has something to do with it.

Gahan Wilson's cartoons have appeared in *Playboy*, *The New Yorker*, *Weird Tales*, *Gourmet*, *Punch*, *Paris Match*, and *The National Lampoon*. Fifteen compilations of his work have been published. *Still Weird*, a career-spanning collection, includes over one hundred new cartoons plus more than three hundred cartoons selected from earlier volumes.

Wilson has written and illustrated children's books, including *The Bang Bang Family*, a picture book, and two *Harry, the Fat Bear Spy* adventures.

For adults, Wilson has written two mystery novels, *Eddy Deco's Last Caper* and *Everybody's Favorite Duck*, and a number of horror short stories, which have appeared in *Playboy*, *Omni*, *The Magazine of Fantasy & Science Fiction*, and numerous anthologies.

Recent projects include graphic novels based on the works of Ambrose Bierce and Edgar Allan Poe, a set of trading cards featuring Wilson's demonic baseball players, and his first animated work, a cartoon short, "Gahan Wilson's Diner," released by 20th Century–Fox.

Wilson is presently working on a feature film for Steven Spielberg's Amblin Entertainment, a TV special for Disney, and an animated sitcom for Universal Pictures.